DOG

DUC

BIT

HEN

THE GRUMPY MORNING

Pamela Duncan Edwards

ILLUSTRATED BY Darcia Labrosse

Hyperion Books for Children
NEW YORK

For information address Hyperion Books for Children,
114 Fifth Avenue, New York, New York 10011-5690.

Printed in Hong Kong by South China Printing Company.

FIRST EDITION
1 3 5 7 9 10 8 6 4 2

The artwork for each picture is prepared using Schminke watercolors
on Papier Special.
This book is set in 20-point Egyptienne Bold.

Library of Congress Cataloging-in-Publication Data

Edwards, Pamela Duncan.
The grumpy morning / Pamela Duncan Edwards ; illustrated by Darcia Labrosse—1st ed.
p. cm.
Summary: A cow's moo sets off a chain reaction
in which the other animals on the farm speak out in their own way
to let the farmer know she is late to feed them.
ISBN 0-7868-0331-2 (trade)—ISBN 0-7868-2279-1 (lib. bdg.)
[1. Domestic animals—Fiction. 2. Stories in rhyme.]
I. Labrosse, Darcia, ill. II. Title.
PZ8.3.E283Qu 1998
[E]—dc20 96-43062

For James Peter Ellison Lawley—
to celebrate your first birthday,
March 28, 1998

—P. D. E.

For my sister Lérie

—D. L.

I heard a cow begin to moo,
"I need to be milked! I really do."

She mooed at the dog, who began to bark,
"It's time for breakfast. It's no longer dark."

I heard a goat begin to bleat,
"Where are my oats?" and she stamped her feet.

She stamped at the hog, who began to squeal,
"I'm waiting for slop. I'm due for a meal."

I heard a rabbit begin to thump,
"I want my pellets. I'll never grow plump."

He thumped at the horse, who began to neigh,
"I'm hungry. I'm hungry. I'm hungry for hay."

I heard a duck begin to quack,
"What's going on? I must have my snack."

She quacked at the cat, who began to meow,
"I'd like a cuddle. I'd like it now."

I heard a hen begin to cluck,
"My grain is late. That's just my luck."

Naa-naa-aa
M-o-o-o
Woof
Quac

Thump-thump
Neigh
21
Cluck
Oink
Meow

I saw a moth land on the nose
Of the sleepy farmer, still in a doze.

She opened an eye and said with a cry,
“Is that the time? Oh, my! Oh, my!

“Good morning, cow.
Good morning, dog.
Good morning, goat.
Good morning, hog.

"Good morning, rabbit.
Good morning, horse.
And duck and cat and owl, of course.
Such a HAPPY morning, isn't it, hen?"

Then she fed them

And milked them

And loved us,
All ten!

May I sleep now?

GOAT
CAT
HOG
ME
HORSE